To Kalera
~G. N.

To Laura and Imogen
~S. A.

Text copyright © 1997 by Grace Nichols
Illustrations copyright © 1997 by Sarah Adams

First U.S. edition 1997

Library of Congress
Cataloging-in-Publication Data

Nichols, Grace, date.
Asana and the animals / Grace Nichols ;
illustrated by Sarah Adams.—1st ed.
Summary: In this collection of poems,
a little girl named Asana describes a
variety of animals—from cats to
hedgehogs to cows.
ISBN 0-7636-0145-4
1. Animals—Juvenile poetry. 2. Children's
poetry, Guyanese.   [1. Animals—Poetry.
2. Blacks—Poetry.   3. Guyanese Poetry.]
I. Adams, Sarah (Sarah L.), ill.   II. Title.
PR9320.9.N45A915 1997 811—dc20
96-30307

10 9 8 7 6 5 4 3 2 1

Printed in Italy

This book was typeset in ITC Highlander Bold.
The pictures were done in oil-based inks, using
colored linocuts.

Candlewick Press
2067 Massachusetts Avenue
Cambridge, Massachusetts 02140

ASANA
AND THE
ANIMALS
A Book of Pet Poems

Grace Nichols

illustrated by **Sarah Adams**

CANDLEWICK PRESS
CAMBRIDGE, MASSACHUSETTS

PIT-A-PAT-A-PARROT

Pit-a-pat-a-parrot
on her parrot back
pit a little pat a little
don't forget to scratch
a little
don't forget to chat
a little
she will learn the knack
a little

If you pit-a-pat-a-parrot
if you chit-a-chat-a-parrot
while you scritch and scratch a parrot

She will chit and chat right back.

LITTLE ASANA

Little Asana sat on a sofa
eating her peas and rice.
There came a small spider
who snuggled up beside her
and Asana said, "I think you're nice."

Now, little Asana is a spider liker,
little Asana is a spider minder,
she always keeps one close beside her.
And sometimes when she's asleep
and dreaming
her spider will take her for
a ride to the ceiling.

What Asana Wanted for Her Birthday

Please don't get me
a hamster or budgie.
Please don't get me
a goldfish or canary.

Please get me something
a little scary.
Maybe something
a wee bit hairy.

How about a tarantula?
What's wrong with a spider pet?
If it gets sick of course
I'll take it to scare—
I mean, to see—
the vet.

MY GRANDMOTHER'S CAT

Why does my grandmother always sit
with her cat in her lap?

Why does my grandmother always sit
stroking that soft, furry back?

Whenever I ask my grandmother why,
she just gives a happy sort of sigh:
"Asana, child,
   it gives me such pleasure,
      then again, it's very, very good
         for my blood pressure."

GRASSHOPPER ONE

Grasshopper one
Grasshopper two
Grasshopper hopping
in the morning dew

Grasshopper three
Grasshopper four
Grasshopper stopping
by the leafy door

Grasshopper five
Grasshopper six
Grasshopper lying
like a green
matchstick

Grasshopper seven
Grasshopper eight
Grasshopper suddenly
standing up straight

Grasshopper nine
Grasshopper ten
Grasshopper,
    will you be my
        secret friend?

DON'T CRY, CATERPILLAR

Don't cry, Caterpillar,
Caterpillar, don't cry
You'll be a butterfly
by and by.

Caterpillar, please
don't worry 'bout a thing—

"But," said the caterpillar,
"will I still know myself
in wings?"

EVERY TIME I SEE HER

She's a slow-plodding
chew-cudding Jersey cow
But every time I see her
I got to go—WOW!

She's calm, she's kind
She's so serene—
She's Ruler of the Pasture,
She's Queen of the Green.

Every time I see her
I just have to think—
What would be my cornflakes
without her milk?

What would be my pudding
without her cream?
She really is
a queen supreme.

She's a lovely buttery
lottery-winning cow
And every time I see her
I got to go—WOW!

DEAR HONEYBEE

Dear Honeybee,
if I speak politely
will you still sting me?

I love the way
you dress
in your black and yellow vest

I love your
see-through wings
and everything

I love your creepy legs
(no, not creepy
just nice and shimmery)

See, Honeybee,
I'm coming . . .
a little closer

But no,
I think I'd better go
back inside, Honeybee,

Good-bye.

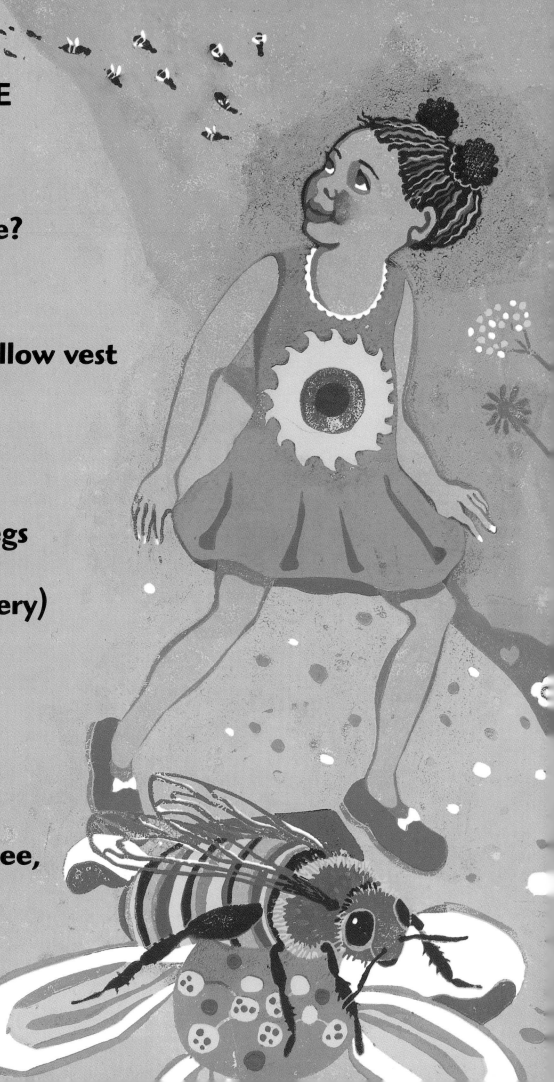

LADYBUG

Red black-spotted Ladybug,
Can you do the jitterbug?

"I've never tried the jitterbug
But when the sunlight hits my wings
You should see me do my thing,
Child, you should see me
do the Glitterbug."

HEY DIDDLE-DIDDLE

Hey diddle-diddle
the cat's on my middle
and my grandma's in the kitchen
with the spoons.

And I can't lift her off
'cause she's digging in her claws.

Grandma, stop the twiddle
and take your cat from my middle.

She doesn't give a fiddle
that I want to get up
and see the moon.

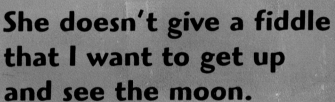

WHAT ASANA SAID ABOUT THE ELEPHANTS AT THE ZOO:

Elephants are nice
because they like
to squirt themselves
with mud and dust
to protect their skin from the sun
then later on they wash it off
in splashing fun.

Can't I be a bit like the elephants, Mom?
I hate putting sunblock on.

LYING STILL IN MUDDY RIVER

Alligator
grey-green
creature
lying still
in muddy river

Pretending to be tree trunk
but I can see your bumpety-bumps
and your long, long mouth
and your half-moon eye
suddenly opening sly

Alligator
grey-green
creature
lying still
in muddy river

Not me, Asana, for your dinner.

HAVE YOU EVER SEEN?

Have you ever seen
a blue tadpole?
Have you ever seen
a spoiled-brat toad?

Have you ever seen
a walking fish?
Have you ever seen
a tricycling chick?

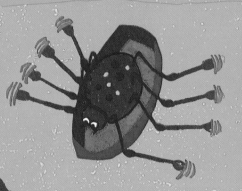

Have you ever seen
a rowing spider?
Have you ever seen
a dancing tiger?

Have you ever seen
a reading parrot?
Have you ever seen
a jogging ocelot?

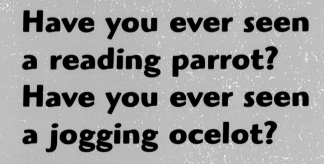

Have you ever?

THREE LITTLE PIGS

Three little pigs starting out all new,
Three little pigs all wondering what to do,
The first built a house of straw,
Wolf . . . there were two!

Two little pigs dragging their feet along,
Two little pigs singing a sad song,
The second built a house of sticks,
Wolf . . . there was one!

One little pig thinking kinda quick,
One little pig going for brick,
He built a house all sturdy and thick,
Wolf . . . huffed-puffed till his old jaws clicked!

Next morning the newspaper said:

CLEVER PIG GOT BAD WOLF LICKED.

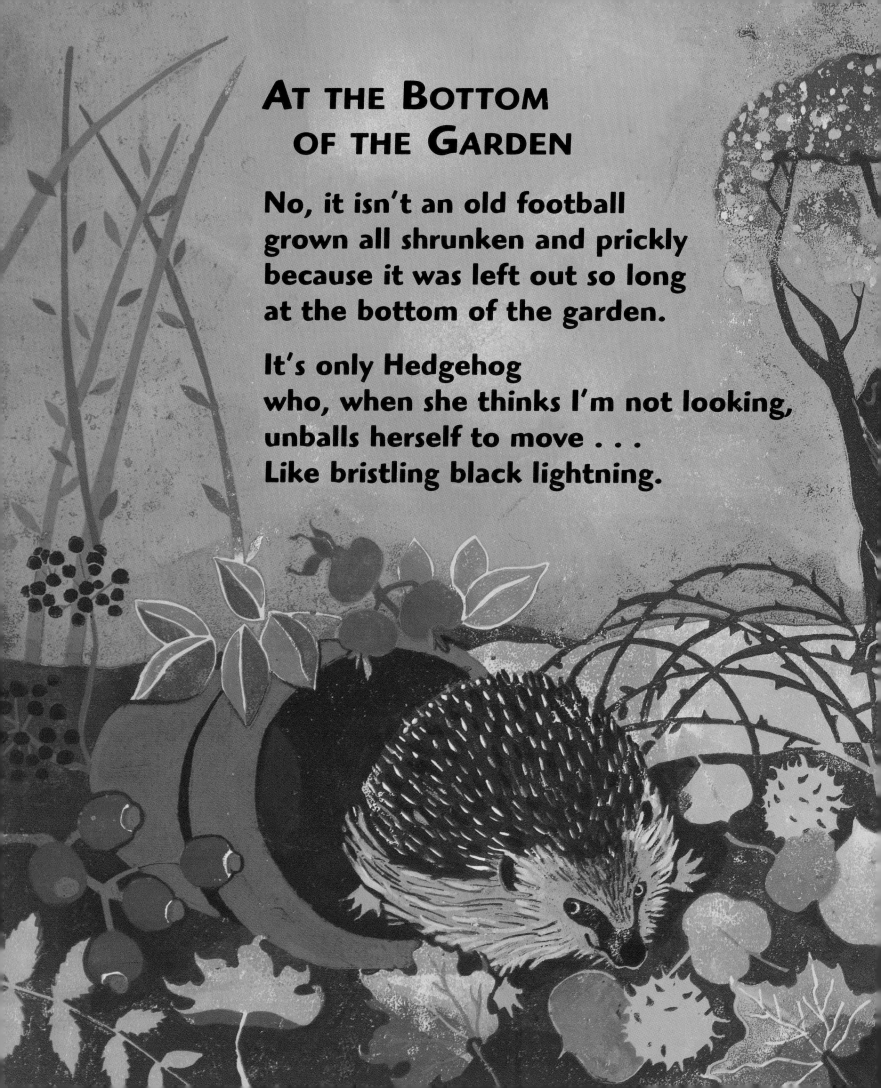

AT THE BOTTOM OF THE GARDEN

No, it isn't an old football
grown all shrunken and prickly
because it was left out so long
at the bottom of the garden.

It's only Hedgehog
who, when she thinks I'm not looking,
unballs herself to move . . .
Like bristling black lightning.

If I Had a Giraffe

If I had a giraffe—
I'd climb up a ladder to her with a laugh.
I'd rest my head against her long neck,
And we'd go—riding riding riding.

We'd go anywhere under the sky,
Maybe to some faraway blue seaside,
Just to see flying fish flashing by,
And we'd go—riding riding riding.

We'd go to the land
where all fruit trees grow,
And my giraffe would stretch her neck
To get me to the highest, rosiest mango,
And we'd go—riding riding riding.

Even to the desert where the hot sands glow,
We'd go—riding riding riding—
Me and my beautiful giraffe friend,
Whose face reminds me of a camel.

Things I Like in the Sea That Go By Swimmingly

Jellyfish
Starfish
Flying fish
Seals

Dolphins
Octopuses
Otters
Eels

Crabs
Turtles
Weevers
Manatees

Sea lions
Walruses
Shrimps
Whales

But best of all
I like Mermaids